Classic Ghost Stories

PENGUIN BOOKS

PENGUIN BOOKS

Published by the Penguin Group
Penguin Books Ltd, 27 Wrights Lane, London W8 5TZ, England
Penguin Books USA Inc., 375 Hudson Street, New York, New York 10014, USA
Penguin Books Australia Ltd, Ringwood, Victoria, Australia
Penguin Books Canada Ltd, 10 Alcorn Avenue, Toronto, Ontario, Canada M4V 3B2
Penguin Books (NZ) Ltd, 182–190 Wairau Road, Auckland 10, New Zealand

Penguin Books Ltd, Registered Offices: Harmondsworth, Middlesex, England

First published 1996
1 3 5 7 9 10 8 6 4 2

This collection copyright © Penguin Books Ltd, 1996
All rights reserved

Set in 12/15pt Monophoto Bembo
Typeset by Datix International Limited, Bungay, Suffolk
Printed in England by Clays Ltd, St Ives plc

Except in the United States of America, this book is sold subject to the condition
that it shall not, by way of trade or otherwise, be lent, re-sold, hired out, or otherwise circulated without the publisher's prior consent in any form of binding or cover
other than that in which it is published and without a similar condition including
this condition being imposed on the subsequent purchaser

Contents

CHARLES DICKENS

The Signal–Man

'HALLOA! Below there!'

When he heard a voice thus calling to him, he was standing at the door of his box, with a flag in his hand, furled round its short pole. One would have thought, considering the nature of the ground, that he could not have doubted from what quarter the voice came; but, instead of looking up to where I stood on the top of the steep cutting nearly over his head, he turned himself about and looked down the line. There was something remarkable in his manner of doing so, though I could not have said, for my life, what. But, I know it was remarkable enough to attract my notice, even though his figure was fore-shortened and shadowed, down in the deep trench, and mine was high above him, so steeped in the glow of an angry sunset that I had shaded my eyes with my hand before I saw him at all.

'Halloa! Below!'

From looking down the line, he turned himself about again, and, raising his eyes, saw my figure high above him.

'Is there any path by which I can come down and speak to you?'

He looked up at me without replying, and I looked down at him without pressing him too soon with a repetition of my idle question. Just then, there came a vague vibration in the earth and air, quickly changing into a violent pulsation, and an oncoming rush that caused me to start back, as though it had force to draw me down. When such vapour as rose to my height from this rapid train, had passed me and was skimming away over the landscape, I looked down again, and saw him re-furling the flag he had shown while the train went by.

I repeated my inquiry. After a pause, during which he seemed to regard me with fixed attention, he motioned with his rolled-up flag towards a point on my level, some two or three hundred yards distant. I called down to him, 'All right!' and made for that point. There, by dint of looking closely about me, I found a rough zig-zag descending path notched out: which I followed.

The cutting was extremely deep, and unusually precipitate. It was made through a clammy stone that became oozier and wetter as I went down. For these reasons, I found the way long enough to give me time to recall a singular air of reluctance or compulsion with which he had pointed out the path.

When I came down low enough upon the zig-zag descent, to see him again, I saw that he was standing between the rails on the way by which the train had lately passed, in an attitude as if he were waiting for me to appear. He had his left hand at his chin, and that left elbow rested on his right hand crossed over his breast. His attitude was one of such expectation and watchfulness, that I stopped for a moment, wondering at it.

I resumed my downward way, and, stepping out upon the level of the railroad and drawing nearer to him, saw that he was a dark sallow man, with a dark beard and rather heavy eyebrows. His post was in as solitary and dismal a place as ever I saw. On either side, a dripping-wet wall of jagged stone, excluding all view but a strip of sky; the perspective one way, only a crooked prolongation of this great dungeon; the shorter perspective in the other direction, terminating in a gloomy red light, and the gloomier entrance to a black tunnel, in whose massive architecture there was a barbarous, depressing, and forbidding air. So little sunlight ever found its way to this spot, that it had an earthy deadly smell; and so much cold wind rushed through it, that it struck chill to me, as if I had left the natural world.

Before he stirred, I was near enough to him to have touched him. Not even then removing his eyes from mine, he stepped back one step, and lifted his hand.

This was a lonesome post to occupy (I said), and it had riveted my attention when I looked down from up yonder. A visitor was a rarity, I should suppose; not an unwelcome rarity, I hoped? In me, he merely saw a man who had been shut up within narrow 4 limits all his life, and who, being at last set free, had a newly-awakened interest in these great works. To such purpose I spoke to him; but I am far from sure of the terms I used, for, besides that I am not happy in opening any conversation, there was something in the man that daunted me.

He directed a most curious look towards the red light near the tunnel's mouth, and looked all about it, as if something were missing from it, and then looked at me.

That light was part of his charge? Was it not?

He answered in a low voice: 'Don't you know it is?'

The monstrous thought came into my mind as I perused the fixed eyes and the saturnine face, that this was a spirit, not a man. I have speculated since, whether there may have been infection in his mind.

In my turn, I stepped back. But in making the action, I detected in his eyes some latent fear of me. This put the monstrous thought to flight.

'You look at me,' I said, forcing a smile, 'as if you had a dread of me.'

'I was doubtful,' he returned, 'whether I had seen you before.'

'Where?'

He pointed to the red light he had looked at.

'There?' I said.

Intently watchful of me, he replied (but without sound), Yes.

'My good fellow, what should I do there? However, be that as it may, I never was there, you may swear.'

'I think I may,' he rejoined. 'Yes. I am sure I may.'

His manner cleared, like my own. He replied to my remarks with readiness, and in well-chosen words. Had he much to do there? Yes; that was to say, he had enough responsibility to bear; but exactness and watchfulness were what was required of him, and of actual work – manual labour he had next to none. To change that signal, to trim those lights, and to turn this iron handle now and then, was all he had to do under that head. Regarding those many long and lonely hours of which I seemed to make so much, he could only say that the routine of his life had shaped itself into that form, and he had grown used to it. He had taught himself a language down here – if only to know it by sight, and to have formed his own crude ideas of its pronunciation, could be called learning it. He had also worked at fractions and decimals, and tried a little algebra; but he was, and had been as a boy, a poor hand at figures. Was it necessary for him when on duty, always to remain in that channel of damp air, and could he never rise into the sunshine from between those high stone walls? Why, that depended upon times and circumstances. Under some conditions there would be less upon the line than under others, and the same held good as to certain hours of the day and night. In bright weather, he did choose occasions for getting a little above these lower shadows; but, being at all times liable to be called by his electric bell, and at such times listening for it with re-doubled anxiety, the relief was less than I would suppose.

He took me into his box, where there was a fire, a desk for an official book in which he had to make certain entries, a telegraphic instrument with its dial face and needles, and the little bell of which he had spoken. On my trusting that he would excuse the remark that he had been well-educated, and (I hoped I might say without offence) perhaps educated above that station, he observed that instances of slight incongruity in such-wise would rarely be found wanting among large bodies of men; that he had heard it was so in workhouses, in the police force, even in that last desperate resource, the army; and that he knew it was so, more or less, in any great railway staff. He had been, when young (if I could believe it, sitting in that hut; he scarcely could), a student of natural philosophy, and had attended lectures; but he had run wild, misused his opportunities, gone down, and never risen again. He had no complaint to offer about that. He had made his bed, and he lay upon it. It was far too late to make another.

All that I have here condensed, he said in a quiet manner, with his grave dark regards divided between me and the fire. He threw in the word 'Sir' from time to time, and especially when he referred to his youth: as though to request me to understand that he claimed to be nothing but what I found him. He was 8 several times interrupted by the little bell, and had to read off messages, and send replies. Once, he had to stand without the door, and display a flag as a train passed, and make some verbal communication to the driver. In the discharge of his duties I observed him to be remarkably exact and vigilant, breaking off his discourse at a syllable, and remaining silent until what he had to do was done.

In a word, I should have set this man down as one of the safest of men to be employed in that capacity, but for the circumstance that while he was speaking to me he twice broke off with a fallen colour, turned his face towards the little bell when it did *not* ring, opened the door of the hut (which was kept shut to exclude the unhealthy damp), and looked out towards the red light near the mouth of the tunnel. On both of those occasions, he came back to the fire with the inexplicable air upon him which I had remarked, without being able to define, when we were so far asunder.

Said I when I rose to leave him: 'You almost make me think that I have met with a contented man.'

(I am afraid I must acknowledge that I said it to lead him on.)

'I believe I used to be so,' he rejoined, in the low voice in which he had first spoken; 'but I am troubled, sir, I am troubled.'

He would have recalled the words if he could. He had said them, however, and I took them up quickly.

'With what? What is your trouble?'

'It is very difficult to impart, sir. It is very, very difficult to speak of. If ever you make me another visit, I will try to tell you.'

'But I expressly intend to make you another visit. Say, when shall it be?'

'I go off early in the morning, and I shall be on again at ten tomorrow night, sir.'

'I will come at eleven.'

He thanked me, and went out at the door with me. 'I'll show my white light, sir,' he said, in his peculiar low voice, 'till you have found the way up. When you have found it, don't call out! And when you are at the top, don't call out!

His manner seemed to make the place strike colder to me, but I said no more than 'Very well.'

'And when you come down tomorrow night, don't

call out! Let me ask you a parting question. What made you cry "Halloa! Below there!" tonight?'

'Heaven knows,' said I. 'I cried something to that effect . . .'

'Not to that effect, sir. Those were the very words. I know them well.'

'Admit those were the very words. I said them, no doubt, because I saw you below.'

'For no other reason?'

'What other reason could I possibly have!'

'You had no feeling that they were conveyed to you in any supernatural way?'

'No.'

He wished me good night, and held up his light. I walked by the side of the down line of rails (with a very disagreeable sensation of a train coming behind me), until I found the path. It was easier to mount than to descend, and I got back to my inn without any adventure.

Punctual to my appointment, I placed my foot on the first notch of the zig-zag next night, as the distant clocks were striking eleven. He was waiting for me at the bottom, with his white light on. 'I have not called out,' I said, when we came close together; 'may I speak now?' 'By all means, sir.' 'Goodnight then, and here's my hand.' 'Goodnight, sir, and here's mine.' With that, we walked side by side to his box, entered it, closed the door, and sat down by the fire.

'I have made up my mind, sir,' he began, bending forward as soon as we were seated, and speaking in a tone but a little above a whisper, 'that you shall not have to ask me twice what troubles me. I took you for someone else yesterday evening. That troubles me.'

'That mistake?'

'No. That someone else.'

'Who is it?'

'I don't know.'

'Like me?'

'I don't know. I never saw the face. The left arm is across the face, and the right arm is waved. Violently waved. This way.'

I followed his action with my eyes, and it was the action of an arm gesticulating with the utmost passion and vehemence: 'For God's sake clear the way!'

'One moonlight night,' said the man, 'I was sitting here, when I heard a voice cry "Halloa! Below there!" I started up, looked from that door, and saw this Someone else standing by the red light near the tunnel, waving as I just now showed you. The voice seemed hoarse with shouting, and it cried, "Look out! Look out!" And then again "Halloa! Below there! Look out!" I caught up my lamp, turned it on red, and ran towards the figure, calling, "What's wrong? What has happened? Where?" It stood just outside the blackness of the tunnel. I advanced so close upon it that I wondered at its keeping the sleeve across its eyes. I ran right up at it, and had my hand stretched out to pull the sleeve away, when it was gone.'

'Into the tunnel,' said I.

'No. I ran on into the tunnel, five hundred yards. I stopped and held my lamp above my head, and saw the figures of the measured distance, and saw the wet stains stealing down the walls and trickling through the arch. I ran out again, faster than I had run in (for I had a mortal abhorrence of the place upon me), and I looked all round the red light with my own red light, and I went up the iron ladder to the gallery atop of it, and I came down again, and ran back here. I telegraphed both ways, "An alarm has been given. Is anything wrong?" The answer came back, both ways: "All well."'

Resisting the slow touch of a frozen finger tracing out my spine, I showed him how that this figure must be a deception of his sense of sight, and how that figures, originating in disease of the delicate nerves that minister to the functions of the eye, were known to have often troubled patients, some of whom had become conscious of the nature of their affliction, and had even proved it by experiments upon themselves. 'As to an imaginary cry,' said I, 'do but listen for a moment to the wind in this unnatural valley while we speak so low, and to the wild harp it makes of the telegraph wires!'

That was all very well, he returned, after we had sat listening for a while, and he ought to know something of the wind and the wires, he who so often passed long winter nights there, alone and watching. But he would beg to remark that he had not finished.

14

I asked his pardon, and he slowly added these words, touching my arm:

'Within six hours after the Appearance, the memorable accident on this line happened, and within ten hours the dead and wounded were brought along through the tunnel over the spot where the figure had stood.'

A disagreeable shudder crept over me, but I did my best against it. It was not to be denied, I rejoined, that this was a remarkable coincidence, calculated deeply to impress his mind. But it was unquestionable that remarkable coincidences did continually occur, and they must be taken into account in dealing with such a subject. Though to be sure I must admit, I added (for I thought I saw that he was going to bring the objection to bear upon me), men of common sense did not allow much for coincidences in making the ordinary calculations of life.

He again begged to remark that he had not finished.

I again begged his pardon for being betrayed into interruptions.

'This,' he said, again laying his hand upon my arm,

and glancing over his shoulder with hollow eyes, 'was just a year ago. Six or seven months passed, and I had recovered from the surprise and shock, when one morning, as the day was breaking, I, standing at that door, looked towards the red light, and saw the spectre again.' He stopped, with a fixed look at me.

'Did it cry out?'

'No. It was silent.'

'Did it wave its arm?'

'No. It leaned against the shaft of the light, with both hands before the face. Like this.'

Once more, I followed his action with my eyes. It was an action of mourning. I have seen such an attitude in stone figures on tombs.

'Did you go up to it?'

'I came in and sat down, partly to collect my thoughts, partly because it had turned me faint. When I went to the door again, daylight was above me, and the ghost was gone.

'But nothing followed? Nothing came of this?'

He touched me on the arm with his forefinger
twice or thrice, giving a ghastly nod each time:

'That very day, as a train came out of the tunnel, I noticed, at a carriage window on my side, what looked like a confusion of hands and heads, and something waved. I saw it, just in time to signal the driver, Stop! He shut off, and put his brake on, but the train drifted past here a hundred and fifty yards or more. I ran after it, and, as I went along, heard terrible screams and cries. A beautiful young lady had died instantaneously in one of the compartments, and was brought in here, and laid down on this floor between us.'

Involuntarily, I pushed my chair back, as I looked from the boards at which he pointed, to himself.

'True, sir. True. Precisely as it happened, so I tell it you.'

I could think of nothing to say, to any purpose, and my mouth was very dry. The wind and the wires took up the story with a long lamenting wail.

He resumed. 'Now, sir, mark this, and judge how my mind is troubled. The spectre came back, a week ago. Ever since, it has been there, now and again, by fits and starts.'

'At the light?'

'At the danger-light.'

'What does it seem to do?'

He repeated, if possible with increased passion and vehemence, that former gesticulation of 'For God's sake clear the way!'

Then, he went on. 'I have no peace or rest for it. It calls to me, for many minutes together, in an agonized manner, "Below there! Look out! Look out!" It stands waving to me. It rings my little bell . . .'

I caught at that. 'Did it ring your bell yesterday evening when I was here, and you went to the door?'

'Twice.'

'Why, see,' said I, 'how your imagination misleads you. My eyes were on the bell, and my ears were open to the bell, and if I am a living man, it did *not* ring at those times. No, nor at any other time, except when it was rung in the natural course of physical things by the station communicating with you.'

He shook his head. 'I have never made a mistake as to that, yet, sir. I have never confused the spectre's ring with the man's. The ghost's ring is a strange vibration in the bell that it derives from nothing else, and I have not asserted that the bell stirs to the eye. I don't wonder that you failed to hear it. But *I* heard it.'

'And did the spectre seem to be there, when you looked out?'

'It *was* there.'

'Both times?'

He repeated firmly: 'Both times.'

'Will you come to the door with me, and look for it now?'

He bit his under-lip as though he were somewhat unwilling, but arose. I opened the door, and stood on the step, while he stood in the doorway. There, was the danger-light. There, was the dismal mouth of the tunnel. There, were the high wet stone walls of the cutting. There, were the stars above them.

'Do you see it?' I asked him, taking particular note of his face. His eyes were prominent and strained; but not very much more so, perhaps, than my own had been when I had directed them earnestly towards the same spot.

'No,' he answered. 'It is not there.'

'Agreed,' said I.

We went in again, shut the door, and resumed our seats. I was thinking how best to improve this advantage, if it might be called one, when he took up the conversation in such a matter of course way, so assuming that there could be no serious question of fact between us, that I felt myself placed in the weakest of positions.

'By this time you will fully understand, sir,' he said, 'that what troubles me so dreadfully, is the question, What does the spectre mean?'

I was not sure, I told him, that I did fully understand.

'What is its warning against?' he said, ruminating, with his eyes on the fire, and only by times turning them on me. 'What is the danger? Where is the danger? There is danger overhanging, somewhere on the line. Some dreadful calamity will happen. It is not to be doubted this third time, after what has gone before. But surely this is a cruel haunting of *me*. What can *I* do?'

20

He pulled out his handkerchief, and wiped the drops from his heated forehead.

'If I telegraph Danger, on either side of me, or on both, I can give no reason for it,' he went on, wiping the palms of his hands. 'I should get into trouble, and do no good. They would think I was mad. This is the way it would work: – Message: "Danger! Take care!" Answer: "What danger? Where?" Message: "Don't know. But for God's sake take care!" They would displace me. What else could they do?'

His pain of mind was most pitiable to see. It was the mental torture of a conscientious man, oppressed beyond endurance by an unintelligible responsibility involving life.

'When it first stood under the danger-light,' he went on, putting his dark hair back from his head, and drawing his hands outward across and across his temples in an extremity of feverish distress, 'why not tell me where that accident was to happen – if it must happen? Why not tell me how it could be averted – if it could have been averted? When on its second coming it hid its face, why not tell me instead: "She 21 is going to die. Let them keep her at home"? If it came, on those two occasions, only to show me that its warnings were true, and so to prepare me for the third, why not warn me plainly now? And I, Lord help me! A mere poor signal-man on this solitary station! Why not go to somebody with credit to be believed, and power to act!'

When I saw him in this state, I saw that for the poor man's sake, as well as for the public safety, what I had to do for the time was to compose his mind. Therefore, setting aside all question of reality or unreality between us, I represented to him that whoever thoroughly discharged his duty, must do well, and that at least it was his comfort that he understood his duty, though he did not understand these confounding Appearances. In this effort I succeeded far better than in the attempt to reason him out of his conviction. He became calm; the occupations incidental to his post as the night advanced, began to make larger demands on his attention; and I left him at two in the morning. I had offered to stay through the
22 night, but he would not hear of it.

That I more than once looked back at the red light as I ascended the pathway, that I did not like the red light, and that I should have slept but poorly if my bed had been under it, I see no reason to conceal. Nor did I like the two sequences of the accident and the dead girl. I see no reason to conceal that, either.

But, what ran most in my thoughts was the consideration how ought I to act, having become the recipient of this disclosure? I had proved the man to be intelligent, vigilant, painstaking, and exact; but how long might he remain so, in his state of mind? Though in a subordinate position, still he held a most important trust, and would I (for instance) like to stake my own life on the chances of his continuing to execute it with precision?

Unable to overcome a feeling that there would be something treacherous in my communicating what he had told me to his superiors in the Company, without first being plain with himself and proposing a middle course to him, I ultimately resolved to offer to accompany him (otherwise keeping his secret for the present) to the wisest medical practitioner we 23 could hear of in those parts, and to take his opinion. A change in his time of duty would come round next night, he had apprised me, and he would be off an hour or two after sunrise, and on again soon after sunset. I had appointed to return accordingly.

Next evening was a lovely evening, and I walked out early to enjoy it. The sun was not yet quite down when I traversed the field-path near the top of the deep cutting. I would extend my walk for an hour, I said to myself, half an hour on and half an hour back, and it would then be time to go to my signal-man's box.

Before pursuing my stroll, I stepped to the brink, and mechanically looked down, from the point from which I had first seen him. I cannot describe the thrill that seized upon me, when, close at the mouth of the tunnel, I saw the appearance of a man, with his left sleeve across his eyes, passionately waving his right arm.

The nameless horror that oppressed me passed in a moment, for in a moment I saw that this appearance 24 of a man was a man indeed, and that there was a little group of other men standing at a short distance, to whom he seemed to be rehearsing the gesture he made. The danger-light was not yet lighted. Against its shaft, a little low hut, entirely new to me, had been made of some wooden supports and tarpaulin. It looked no bigger than a bed.

With an irresistible sense that something was wrong – with a flashing self-reproachful fear that fatal mischief had come of my leaving the man there, and causing no one to be sent to overlook or correct what he did – I descended the notched path with all the speed I could make.

'What is the matter?' I asked the men.

'Signal-man killed this morning, sir.'

'Not the man belonging to that box?'

'Yes, sir.'

'Not the man I know?'

'You will recognize him, sir, if you knew him,' said the man who spoke for the others, solemnly uncovering his own head and raising an end of the tarpaulin, 'for his face is quite composed.'

'Oh! how did this happen, how did this happen?' I

asked, turning from one to another as the hut closed in again.

'He was cut down by an engine, sir. No man in England knew his work better. But somehow he was not clear of the outer rail. It was just at broad day. He had struck the light, and had the lamp in his hand. As the engine came out of the tunnel, his back was towards her, and she cut him down. That man drove her, and was showing how it happened. Show the gentleman, Tom.'

The man, who wore a rough dark dress, stepped back to his former place at the mouth of the tunnel!

'Coming round the curve in the tunnel, sir,' he said, 'I saw him at the end, like as if I saw him down a perspective-glass. There was no time to check speed, and I knew him to be very careful. As he didn't seem to take heed of the whistle, I shut it off when we were running down upon him, and called to him as loud as I could call.'

'What did you say?'

'I said, Below there! Look out! Look out! For God's sake clear the way!'

I started.

'Ah! it was a dreadful time, sir. I never left off calling to him. I put this arm before my eyes, not to see, and I waved this arm to the last; but it was no use.'

Without prolonging the narrative to dwell on any one of its curious circumstances more than on any other, I may, in closing it, point out the coincidence that the warning of the Engine-driver included, not only the words which the unfortunate Signal-man had repeated to me as haunting him, but also the words which I myself – not he – had attached, and that only in my own mind, to the gesticulation he had imitated.

The Phantom Ship

THE ship was ready to sail for Europe; and Philip Vanderdecken went on board – hardly caring whither he went. To return to Terneuse was not his object; he could not bear the idea of revisiting the scene of so much happiness and so much misery. Amine's form was engraven on his heart, and he looked forward with impatience to the time when he should be summoned to join her in the land of spirits.

He had awakened as from a dream, after so many years of aberration of intellect. He was no longer the sincere Catholic that he had been; for he never thought of religion without his Amine's cruel fate being brought to his recollection. Still he clung on to the relic – he believed in that – and that only. It was his god – his creed – his everything – the passport for himself and for his father into the next world – the means whereby he should join his Amine – and for

28

hours would he remain holding in his hand that object so valued – gazing upon it – recalling every important event in his life, from the death of his poor mother, and his first sight of Amine; to the last dreadful scene. It was to him a journal of his existence, and on it were fixed all his hopes for the future.

'When! oh, when is it to be accomplished!' was the constant subject of his reveries. 'Blessed, indeed, will be the day when I leave this world of hate, and seek that other in which "the weary are at rest".'

The vessel on board of which Philip was embarked as a passenger was the *Nostra Señora da Monte,* a brig of three hundred tons, bound for Lisbon. The Captain was an old Portuguese, full of superstition, and fond of arrack – a fondness rather unusual with the people of his nation. They sailed from Goa, and Philip was standing abaft, and sadly contemplating the spire of the Cathedral, in which he had last parted with his wife, when his elbow was touched, and he turned round.

'Fellow-passenger again!' said a well-known voice – it was that of the pilot Schriften.

There was no alteration in the man's appearance; he showed no marks of declining years; his one eye glared as keenly as ever.

Philip started, not only at the sight of the man, but at the reminiscences which his unexpected appearance brought to his mind. It was but for a second, and he was again calm and pensive.

'You here again, Schriften?' observed Philip. 'I trust your appearance forebodes the accomplishment of my task.'

'Perhaps it does,' replied the pilot; 'we both are weary.'

Philip made no reply; he did not even ask Schriften in what manner he had escaped from the fort; he was indifferent about it; for he felt that the man had a charmed life.

'Many are the vessels that have been wrecked, Philip Vanderdecken, and many the souls summoned to their account by meeting with your father's ship, while you have been so long shut up,' observed the pilot.

'May our next meeting with him be more fortunate – may it be the last!' replied Philip.

'No, no! rather may he fulfil his doom, and sail till the day of judgement,' replied the pilot with emphasis.

'Vile caitiff! I have a foreboding that you will not have your detestable wish. Away! – leave me! or you shall find that although this head is blanched by misery, this arm has still some power.'

Schriften scowled as he walked away; he appeared to have some fear of Philip, although it was not equal to his hate. He now resumed his former attempts of stirring up the ship's company against Philip, declaring that he was a Jonah, who would occasion the loss of the ship, and that he was connected with *The Flying Dutchman*. Philip very soon observed that he was avoided; and he resorted to counter-statements, equally injurious to Schriften, whom he declared to be a demon. The appearance of Schriften was so much against him, while that of Philip, on the contrary, was so prepossessing, that the people on board hardly knew what to think. They were divided: some were on the side of Philip – some on that of Schriften; the captain and many others looking with equal horror upon both, and longing for the time when they could be sent out of the vessel.

The captain, as we have before observed, was very superstitious, and very fond of his bottle. In the morning he would be sober and pray; in the afternoon he would be drunk, and swear at the very saints whose protection he had invoked but a few hours before.

'May Holy Saint Antonio preserve us, and keep us from temptation,' said he, on the morning after a conversation with the passengers about the Phantom Ship. 'All the saints protect us from harm,' continued he, taking off his hat reverentially, and crossing himself. 'Let me but rid myself of these two dangerous men without accident, and I will offer up a hundred wax candles, of three ounces each, to the shrine of the Virgin, upon my safe anchoring off the tower of Belem.' In the evening he changed his language.

'Now, if that Maldetto Saint Antonio don't help us, may he feel the coals of hell yet; damn him and his pigs too; if he has the courage to do his duty, all will be well; but he is a cowardly wretch, he cares for nobody, and will not help those who call upon him in trouble. Carambo! that for you,' exclaimed the captain, looking at the small shrine of the saint at the bittacle, and snapping his fingers at the image – 'that for you, you useless wretch, who never help us in our trouble. The Pope must canonize some better saints for us, for all we have now are worn out. They could do something formerly, but now I would not give two ounces of gold for the whole calendar; as for you, you lazy old scoundrel,' continued the captain, shaking his fist at poor Saint Antonio.

The ship had now gained off the southern coast of Africa, and was about one hundred miles from the Lagullas coast; the morning was beautiful, a slight ripple only turned over the waves, the breeze was light and steady, and the vessel was standing on a wind, at the rate of about four miles an hour.

'Blessed be the holy saints,' said the captain, who had just gained the deck; 'another little slant in our favour, and we shall lay our course. Again I say, blessed be the holy saints, and particularly our worthy 33 patron Saint Antonio, who has taken under his peculiar protection the *Nostra Señora da Monte*. We have a prospect of fine weather; come, signors, let us down to breakfast, and after breakfast we will enjoy our cigarros upon the deck.'

But the scene was soon changed; a bank of clouds rose up from the eastward, with a rapidity that, to the seamen's eyes, was unnatural, and it soon covered the whole firmament; the sun was obscured, and all was one deep and unnatural gloom; the wind subsided, and the ocean was hushed. It was not exactly dark, but the heavens were covered with one red haze, which gave an appearance as if the world was in a state of conflagration.

In the cabin the increased darkness was first observed by Philip, who went on deck; he was followed by the captain and passengers, who were in a state of amazement. It was unnatural and incomprehensible. 'Now, holy Virgin, protect us – what can this be?' exclaimed the captain in a fright. 'Holy Saint Antonio, protect us – but this is awful.'

34   'There! there!' shouted the sailors, pointing to the

beam of the vessel. Every eye looked over the gunnel to witness what had occasioned such exclamations. Philip, Schriften, and the captain were side by side. On the beam of the ship, not more than two cables' length distant, they beheld, slowly rising out of the water, the tapering masthead and spars of another vessel. She rose, and rose gradually; her top-masts and top-sail yards, with the sails set, next made their appearance; higher and higher she rose up from the element. Her lower masts and rigging, and, lastly, her hull showed itself above the surface. Still she rose up till her ports, with her guns, and at last the whole of her floatage was above water, and there she remained close to them, with her main-yard squared, and hove-to.

'Holy Virgin!' exclaimed the captain, breathless; 'I have known ships to *go down,* but never to *come up* before. Now will I give one thousand candles, of ten ounces each, to the shrine of the Virgin to save us in this trouble. One thousand wax candles! Hear me, blessed lady; ten ounces each. Gentlemen,' cried the captain to the passengers, who stood aghast, 'why don't you promise? Promise, I say; promise, at all events.'

'The Phantom Ship – *The Flying Dutchman*,' shriek-ed Schriften 'I told you so, Philip Vanderdecken; there is your father. He! he!'

Philip's eyes had remained fixed on the vessel; he perceived that they were lowering down a boat from her quarter. 'It is possible,' thought he, 'I shall now be permitted!' and Philip put his hand into his bosom and grasped the relic.

The gloom now increased, so that the strange vessel's hull could but just be discovered through the murky atmosphere. The seamen and passengers threw themselves down on their knees, and invoked their saints. The captain ran down for a candle, to light before the image of Saint Antonio, which he took out of its shrine, and kissed with much apparent affection and devotion, and then replaced.

Shortly afterwards the splash of oars was heard alongside, and a voice calling out, 'I say, my good people, give us a rope from forward.'

No one answered, or complied with the request. Schriften only went up to the captain, and told him that if they offered to send letters they must not be received or the vessel would be doomed, and all would perish.

A man now made his appearance from over the gunnel, at the gangway. 'You might as well have let me have a side rope, my hearties,' said he, as he stepped on deck; 'where is the captain?'

'Here,' replied the captain, trembling from head to foot. The man who accosted him appeared a weather-beaten seaman, dressed in a fur cap and canvas petticoats; he held some letters in his hand.

'What do you want?' at last screamed the captain.

'Yes – what do you want?' continued Schriften. 'He! he!'

'What, you here, pilot?' observed the man; 'well – I thought you had gone to Davy's locker, long enough ago.'

'He! he!' replied Schriften, turning away.

'Why the fact is, captain, we have had very foul weather, and we wish to send letters home; I do believe that we shall never get round this Cape.'

'I can't take them,' cried the captain.

'Can't take them! well, it's very odd – but every

ship refuses to take our letters; it's very unkind — seamen should have a feeling for brother seamen, especially in distress. God knows, we wish to see our wives and families again; and it would be a matter of comfort to them, if they only could hear from us.'

'I cannot take your letters — the saints preserve us,' replied the captain.

'We have been a long while out,' said the seaman, shaking his head.

'How long?' inquired the captain, not knowing what to say.

'We can't tell; our almanack was blown overboard, and we have lost our reckoning. We never have our latitude exact now, for we cannot tell the sun's declination for the right day.'

'Let *me* see your letters,' said Philip, advancing, and taking them out of the seaman's hands.

'They must not be touched,' screamed Schriften.

'Out, monster!' replied Philip, 'who dares interfere with me?'

'Doomed — doomed — doomed!' shrieked Schriften,

running up and down the deck, and then breaking into a wild fit of laughter.

'Touch not the letters,' said the captain, trembling as if in an ague fit.

Philip made no reply, but held his hand out for the letters.

'Here is one from our second mate, to his wife at Amsterdam, who lives on Waser Quay.'

'Waser Quay has long been gone, my good friend; there is now a large dock for ships where it once was,' replied Philip.

'Impossible!' replied the man; 'here is another from the boatswain to his father, who lives in the old market-place.'

'The old market-place has long been pulled down, and there now stands a church upon the spot.'

'Impossible!' replied the seaman; 'here is another from myself to my sweetheart, Vrow Ketser – with money to buy her a new brooch.'

Philip shook his head – 'I remember seeing an old lady of that name buried some thirty years ago.'

'Impossible! I left her young and blooming. Here's

one for the house of Slutz & Co., to whom the ship belongs.'

'There's no such house now,' replied Philip; 'but I have heard that many years ago there was a firm of that name.'

'Impossible! you must be laughing at me. Here is a letter from our captain to his son . . .'

'Give it me,' cried Philip, seizing the letter. He was about to break the seal when Schriften snatched it out of his hand, and threw it over the lee gunnel.

'That's a scurvy trick for an old shipmate,' observed the seaman. Schriften made no reply, but catching up the other letters which Philip had laid down on the capstan, he hurled them after the first.

The strange seaman shed tears, and walked again to the side. 'It is very hard – very unkind,' observed he, as he descended; 'the time may come when you may wish that your family should know your situation.' So saying, he disappeared – in a few seconds was heard the sound of the oars, retreating from the ship.

40 'Holy Saint Antonio!' exclaimed the captain, 'I am

lost in wonder and fright. Steward, bring me up the arrack.'

The steward ran down for the bottle; being as much alarmed as his captain, he helped himself before he brought it up to his commander. 'Now,' said the captain, after keeping his mouth for two minutes to the bottle, and draining it to the bottom, 'what is to be done next?'

'I'll tell you,' said Schriften, going up to him. 'That man there has a charm hung round his neck; take it from him and throw it overboard, and your ship will be saved; if not, it will be lost, with every soul on board.'

'Yes, yes, it's all right, depend on it,' cried the sailors.

'Fools,' replied Philip, 'do you believe that wretch? Did you not hear the man who came on board recognize him, and call him shipmate? He is the party whose presence on board will prove so unfortunate.'

'Yes, yes,' cried the sailors, 'it's all right, the man did call him shipmate.'

'I tell you it's all wrong,' cried Schriften; 'that is the man, let him give up the charm.'

'Yes, yes; let him give up the charm,' cried the sailors, and they rushed upon Philip.

Philip started back to where the captain stood. 'Madmen, know ye what ye are about? It is the holy cross that I wear round my neck. Throw it overboard if you dare, and your souls are lost for ever': and Philip took the relic from his bosom and showed it to the captain.

'No, no, men,' exclaimed the captain, who was now more settled in his nerves; 'that won't do – the saints protect us.'

The seamen, however, became clamorous; one portion were for throwing Schriften overboard, the other for throwing Philip; at last, the point was decided by the captain, who directed the small skiff, hanging astern, to be lowered down, and ordered both Philip and Schriften to get into it. The seamen approved of this arrangement, as it satisfied both parties. Philip made no objection; Schriften screamed and fought, but he was tossed into the boat. There he remained trembling in the stern sheets, while Philip, who had seized the sculls, pulled away from the vessel in the direction of the Phantom Ship.

In a few minutes the vessel which Philip and Schriften had left was no longer to be discerned through the thick haze; the Phantom Ship was still in sight, but at a much greater distance from them than she was before. Philip pulled hard towards her, but although hove-to, she appeared to increase her distance from the boat. For a short time he paused on his oars to regain his breath, when Schriften rose up and took his seat in the stern sheets of the boat. 'You may pull and pull, Philip Vanderdecken,' observed Schriften; 'but you will not gain that ship – no, no, that cannot be – we may have a long cruise together, but you will be as far from your object at the end of it as you are now at the commencement. Why don't you throw me overboard again? You would be all the lighter – He! he!'

'I threw you overboard in a state of frenzy,' replied Philip, 'when you attempted to force from me my relic.'

'And have I not endeavoured to make others take it from you this very day? – Have I not – He! he!'

'You have,' rejoined Philip; 'but I am now convinced, that you are as unhappy as myself, and that in what you are doing, you are only following your destiny, as I am mine. Why and wherefore I cannot tell, but we are both engaged in the same mystery; − if the success of my endeavours depends upon guarding the relic, the success of yours depends upon your obtaining it, and defeating my purpose by so doing. In this matter we are both agents, and you have been, as far as my mission is concerned, my most active enemy. But, Schriften, I have not forgotten, and never will, that you kindly *did advise* my poor Amine; that you prophesied to her what would be her fate, if she did not listen to your counsel; that you were no enemy of hers, although you have been, and are still mine. Although my enemy, for her sake *I forgive you*, and will not attempt to harm you.'

'You do then *forgive your enemy*, Philip Vanderdecken?' replied Schriften, mournfully, 'for such, I acknowledge myself to be.'

'I do, with *all my heart, with all my soul*,' replied
Philip.

'Then you have conquered me, Philip Vanderdecken; you have now made me your friend, and your wishes are about to be accomplished. You would know who I am. Listen: – when your father defying the Almighty's will, in his rage took my life, he was vouchsafed a chance of his doom being cancelled through the merits of his son. I had also my appeal, which was for *vengeance*; it was granted that I should remain on earth, and thwart your will. That as long as we were enemies, you should not succeed; but that when you had conformed to the highest attribute of Christianity, proved on the holy cross, that of *forgiving your enemy*, your task should be fulfilled. Philip Vanderdecken, you have forgiven your enemy, and both our destinies are now accomplished.'

As Schriften spoke, Philip's eyes were fixed upon him. He extended his hand to Philip – it was taken; and as it was pressed, the form of the pilot wasted as it were into the air, and Philip found himself alone.

'Father of Mercy, I thank Thee,' said Philip, 'that my task is done, and that I again may meet my Amine.'

Philip then pulled towards the Phantom Ship, and

found that she no longer appeared to leave him; on the contrary, every minute he was nearer and nearer, and at last he threw in his oars, climbed up her sides, and gained her deck.

The crew of the vessel crowded round him.

'Your captain,' said Philip; 'I must speak with your captain.'

'Who shall I say, sir?' demanded one, who appeared to be the first mate.

'Who?' replied Philip. 'Tell him his son would speak to him, his son Philip Vanderdecken.'

Shouts of laughter from the crew followed this answer of Philip's; and the mate, as soon as they ceased, observed with a smile:

'You forget, sir, perhaps you would say his father.'

'Tell him his son, if you please,' replied Philip; 'take no note of grey hairs.'

'Well, sir, here he is coming forward,' replied the mate, stepping aside, and pointing to the captain.

'What is all this?' inquired the captain.

'Are you Philip Vanderdecken, the captain of this vessel?'

'I am, sir,' replied the other.

'You appear not to know me! But how can you? You saw me but when I was only three years old; yet may you remember a letter which you gave to your wife.'

'Ha!' replied the captain; 'and who then are you?'

'Time has stopped with you, but with those who live in the world he stops not! and for those who pass a life of misery, he hurries on still faster. In me, behold your son, Philip Vanderdecken, who has obeyed your wishes; and after a life of such peril and misery as few have passed, has at last fulfilled his vow, and now offers to his father this precious relic that he required to kiss.'

Philip drew out the relic, and held it towards his father. As if a flash of lightning had passed through his mind, the captain of the vessel started back, clasped his hands, fell on his knees, and wept.

'My son, my son!' exclaimed he, rising, and throwing himself into Philip's arms, 'my eyes are opened – the Almighty knows how long they have been obscured.' Embracing each other, they walked aft, away from the men, who were still crowded at the gangway.

'My son, my noble son, before the charm is broken – before we resolve, as we must, into the elements, oh! let me kneel in thanksgiving and contrition: my son, my noble son, receive a father's thanks,' exclaimed Vanderdecken. Then with tears of joy and penitence he humbly addressed himself to that Being whom he once so awfully defied.

The elder Vanderdecken knelt down: Philip did the same; still embracing each other with one arm, while they raised on high the other, and prayed.

For the last time the relic was taken from the bosom of Philip and handed to his father – and his father raised his eyes to heaven and kissed it. And as he kissed it, the long tapering upper spars of the Phantom vessel, the yards and sails that were set, fell into dust, fluttered in the air and sank upon the wave. Then mainmast, foremast bowsprit, everything above the deck, crumbled into atoms and disappeared.

48   Again he raised the relic to his lips and the work of

destruction continued, the heavy iron guns sank through the decks and disappeared; the crew of the vessel (who were looking on) crumbled down into skeletons, and dust, and fragments of ragged garments; and there were none left on board the vessel in the semblance of life but the father and the son.

Once more did he put the sacred emblem to his lips, and the beams and timber separated, the decks of the vessel slowly sank, and the remnants of the hull floated upon the water; and as the father and son — the one young and vigorous, the other old and decrepit — still kneeling, still embracing, with their hands raised to heaven, sank slowly under the deep blue wave, the lurid sky was for a moment illuminated by a lightning cross.

Then did the clouds which obscured the heavens roll away swift as thought — the sun again burst out in all his splendour — the rippling waves appeared to dance with joy. The screaming seagull again whirled in the air, and the scared albatross once more slumbered on the wing. The porpoise tumbled and tossed in his sportive play, the albicore and dolphin leaped 49 from the sparkling sea. All nature smiled as if it rejoiced that the charm was dissolved for ever, and that the Phantom Ship was no more.

The Ghost-Brahman

ONCE on a time there lived a poor Brahman, who not being a Kulin, found it the hardest thing in the world to get married. He went to rich people and begged of them to give him money that he might marry a wife. And a large sum of money was needed, not so much for the expenses of the wedding, as for giving to the parents of the bride. He begged from door to door, flattered many rich folk, and at last succeeded in scraping together the sum needed. The wedding took place in due time; and he brought home his wife to his mother. After a short time he said to his mother – 'Mother, I have no means to support you and my wife; I must therefore go to distant countries to get money somehow or other. I may be away for years, for I won't return till I get a good sum. In the meantime I'll give you what I have; you make the best of it, and take care of my wife.' 51

The Brahman, receiving his mother's blessing, set out on his travels. In the evening of that very day, a ghost assuming the exact appearance of the Brahman came into the house. The newly-married woman, thinking it was her husband, said to him – 'How is it that you have returned so soon? You said you might be away for years; why have you changed your mind?' The ghost said – 'Today is not a lucky day, I have therefore returned home; besides, I have already got some money.' The mother did not doubt but that it was her son. So the ghost lived in the house as if he was its owner, and as if he was the son of the old woman and the husband of the young woman. As the ghost and the Brahman were exactly like each other in everything, like two peas, the people in the neighbourhood all thought that the ghost was the real Brahman. After some years the Brahman returned from his travels; and what was his surprise when he found another like him in the house. The ghost said to the Brahman – 'Who are you? what business have you to come to *my* house?' 'Who am I?' replied the

Brahman, 'let me ask who you are. This is my house;

that is my mother, and this is my wife.' The ghost said – 'Why herein is a strange thing. Everyone knows that this is my house, that is my wife, and yonder is my mother; and I have lived here for years. And you pretend this is your house, and that woman is your wife. Your head must have got turned, Brahman.' So saying the ghost drove away the Brahman from his house. The Brahman became mute with wonder. He did not know what to do. At last he bethought himself of going to the King and of laying his case before him. The King saw the ghost-Brahman as well as the Brahman, and the one was the picture of the other; so he was in a fix, and did not know how to decide the quarrel. Day after day the Brahman went to the King and besought him to give him back his house, his wife, and his mother; and the King, not knowing what to say every time, put him off to the following day. Every day the King tells him to – 'Come tomorrow'; and every day the Brahman goes away from the palace weeping and striking his forehead with the palm of his hand, and saying – 'What a wicked world this is! I am driven from my own 53 house, and another fellow has taken possession of my house and of my wife! And what a King this is! He does not do justice.'

Now, it came to pass that as the Brahman went away every day from the court outside the town, he passed a spot at which a great many cowboys used to play. They let the cows graze on the meadow, while they themselves met together under a large tree to play. And they played at royalty. One cowboy was elected king; another, prime minister or vizier; another, *kotwal*, or prefect of the police; and others, constables. Every day for several days together they saw the Brahman passing by weeping. One day the cowboy king asked his vizier whether he knew why the Brahman wept every day. On the vizier not being able to answer the question, the cowboy king ordered one of his constables to bring the Brahman to him. One of them went and said to the Brahman – 'The king requires your immediate attendance.' The Brahman replied – 'What for? I have just come from the King, and he put me off till tomorrow. Why 54 does he want me again?' 'It is our king that wants you – our neat-herd king,' rejoined the constable. 'Who is neat-herd king?' asked the Brahman. 'Come and see,' was the reply. The neat-herd king then asked the Brahman why he every day went away weeping. The Brahman then told him his sad story. The neat-herd king, after hearing the whole, said, 'I understand your case; I will give you again all your rights. Only go to the King and ask his permission for me to decide your case.' The Brahman went back to the King of the country, and begged His Majesty to send his case to the neat-herd king, who had offered to decide it. The King, whom the case had greatly puzzled, granted the permission sought. The following morning was fixed for the trial. The neat-herd king, who saw through the whole, brought with him next day a phial with a narrow neck. The Brahman and the ghost-Brahman both appeared at the bar. After a great deal of examination of witnesses and of speech-making, the neat-herd king said – 'Well, I have heard enough. I'll decide the case at once. Here is this phial. Whichever of you will enter into it shall be declared by the court to be the rightful 55 owner of the house, the title of which is in dispute. Now, let me see, which of you will enter.' The Brahman said – 'You are a neat-herd, and your intellect is that of a neat-herd. What man can enter into such a small phial?' 'If you cannot enter,' said the neat-herd king, 'then you are not the rightful owner. What do you say, sir, to this?' turning to the ghost-Brahman and addressing him. 'If you can enter into the phial, then the house and the wife and the mother become yours.' 'Of course I will enter,' said the ghost. And true to his word, to the wonder of all, he made himself into a small creature like an insect, and entered into the phial. The neat-herd king forthwith corked up the phial, and the ghost could not get out. Then, addressing the Brahman, the neat-herd king said, 'Throw this phial into the bottom of the sea, and take possession of your house, wife, and mother.' The Brahman did so, and lived happily for many years and begat sons and daughters.

Penguin Children's 60s

ALI BABA AND THE FORTY THIEVES • *Retold by N. J. Dawood*
THE AMAZING PIPPI LONGSTOCKING • *Astrid Lindgren*
ANNE AT GREEN GABLES • *L. M. Montgomery*
AT THE RIVER-GATES AND
OTHER SUPERNATURAL STORIES • *Philippa Pearce*
CLASSIC GHOST STORIES
CLASSIC NONSENSE VERSE
THE CLOCKWORK MOUSE • *Dick King-Smith*
DEAD MAN'S LANE • *Joan Aiken*
THE DRAGON ON THE ROOF • *Terry Jones*
FOUR GREAT GREEK MYTHS • *Roger Lancelyn Green*
THE GREAT MOUSE PLOT AND
OTHER TALES OF CHILDHOOD • *Roald Dahl*
THE GREAT TIME WARP ADVENTURE • *Jon Scieszka*
THE HOOLIGAN'S SHAMPOO • *Philip Ridley*
KEEP IT IN THE FAMILY • *Anne Fine*
KING ARTHUR'S COURT • *Roger Lancelyn Green*
THE LITTLE MERMAID AND
OTHER FAIRY TALES • *Hans Andersen (Translated by Naomi Lewis)*
LOST DOG AND OTHER STORIES • *Penelope Lively*
THE MIDNIGHT STORY • *Margaret Mahy*
MOOMINTROLLS AND FRIENDS • *Tove Jansson*
MRS PEPPERPOT TURNS DETECTIVE • *Alf Prøysen*
THE NIGHT TRAIN: STORIES IN PROSE AND VERSE • *Allan Ahlberg*
THE PIED PIPER OF HAMELIN AND OTHER CLASSIC STORIES IN VERSE
ROBIN HOOD AND HIS MERRY MEN • *Roger Lancelyn Green*
SHERLOCK HOLMES AND THE SPECKLED BAND • *Sir Arthur Conan Doyle*
SMACKING MY LIPS • *Michael Rosen*
TALES FROM ALICE IN WONDERLAND • *Lewis Carroll*
TALES FROM THE JUNGLE BOOK • *Rudyard Kipling*
THREE QUIRKY TAILS • *Paul Jennings*
TOM SAWYER'S PIRATE ADVENTURE • *Mark Twain*
TOM THUMB AND OTHER FAIRY TALES • *Jacob and Wilhelm Grimm*

Some other books available from Penguin in Puffin Classics

A CHRISTMAS CAROL *Charles Dickens*
DRACULA *Bram Stoker*
FRANKENSTEIN *Mary Shelley*
THE HOUND OF THE BASKERVILLES
Sir Arthur Conan Doyle
THE PHANTOM OF THE OPERA *Gaston Leroux*
THE MYSTERIOUS ADVENTURES OF
SHERLOCK HOLMES *Sir Arthur Conan Doyle*
TALES OF MYSTERY AND TERROR *Edgar Allan Poe*